Eli
and the FRIENDSHIP TALE

Written by *Anna Hinsley*
***Illustrated by* Brooke Slade**

Little
Red
Rocking
Chair
Publishing

Eli
and the FRIENDSHIP TALE

Copyright © 2016 by Anna Hinsley

Illustrations by: Brooke Slade

Book Editing & Design by: Maritza Cosano
Maritza@littleredrockingchair.org
www.littleredrockingchair.org

Little
Red
Rocking
Chair
Publishing

ISBN: 978-0-997-7167-0-2

Book Website
www.eli-tales.com
Email: info@eli-tales.com

Give feedback on the book at:
Anna@eli-tales.com

Printed in U.S.A

To all the kids who will grow to love ELi.

FAR AWAY hidden from

Our **HUMAN** world,

There once was a **JUNGLE**,

Its **VINES** unfurled.

With PYTHONS

That SLITHER

And TREES galore,

With CREATURES that run

And BIRDS that soar.

Deep in those WOODS

Was a CHEETAH so proud,

His growls SHOOK the forest

—powerful AND loud.

His foes FEARED his roar

And he'd always WIN.

Why, once he scared PYTHON

Right out of HIS skin!

Monkeys reached,
SWINGING

To tug at **HIS** ear,

But **CHEETAH** was swift

AND steered his **EARS**

CLEAR.

EVEN the swans

Tried their **SWOOP** and tackle.

But **READY** was **Cheetah,**

Who said with a

CACKLE...

"You poor **LITTLE** creatures,

Can **YOU** not see?

No **ANIMAL** here

Is as smart as **ME!**"

He TAUNTED the swans,

And PYTHON on limb;

For no one in the JUNGLE

Was a match for HIM.

Until, at **LONG** last—

JUST one more did try.

T'was a LARGE elephant

Whose name was ELI.

All watched as he MARCHED

Up To Cheetah's DARK den, with the

THUNDERING

Courage of a

HUNDRED MEN.

Eli came CLOSEST any

DARED to that cave,

Trying to be STRONG,

TRYING to be brave.

Low in **TALL** grass he so

Quietly **SANK**,

And then **HE** gave

Cheetah's **TAIL** a mighty—

YANK!

Eli trumpeted LOUD

And CHEETAH did say,

"You woke me from SLEEP

And NOW you will pay!"

Not thinking it THROUGH.

Like LIGHTNING

Cheetah RAN.

But LITTLE did he know that

ELI had a PLAN.

Claws drawn, CHEETAH

RACED right into a pickle:

That cat jumped HIGH,

TO receive...

A TICKLE!!

After his long, long **LAUGH**,

He had **NOTHING** to say;

For never had **CHEETAH**

Been **TREATED** this way.

Sometimes a good LAUGH,

Or even a GIGGLE,

Can soften a CAT'S pride,

WITH only one tickle.

And so that

CHEETAH,

Who used to be RUDE,

Became KIND,

Changed his MIND,

And his bad, bad MOOD.

But before CHEETAH GOES

AND tells you goodbye,

He'd like to THANK

A LITTLE elephant—

His new friend, ELI.

Anna Hinsley

is a 14-year-old from Parkland, Florida, who lives with her family and golden retriever, Iroquois. She loves to read all things mysterious, and in her spare time sketches and binge-watches Netflix. Occasionally, she attempts yoga, but will never pass up a good smoothie. Anna began writing stories in 2010, and aspires to write many more adventures.

For more **Eli,** visit www.eli-tales.com.

Also available as an ebook.